SWEET TREATS

A BLUEBERRY SPRINGS VALENTINE'S DAY SHORT
STORY ROMANCE BOX SET

JEAN ORAM

Sweet Treats: A Blueberry Springs Valentine's Day Short Story
Romance Box Set
© 2015 Jean Oram

Printed in the United States of America unless otherwise stated on the last page of this book. Published by Oram Productions Alberta, Canada.

Cover by Qamber Designs & Media www.qamberdesignsandmedia.com

LIBRARY OF CONGRESS CATALOGING-IN-PUBLICATION DATA
    Oram, Jean.
    Sweet Treats: A Blueberry Springs Valentine's Day Short Story Romance Box Set / Jean Oram.—1st. ed.
    p. cm.
    ISBN 978-1-928198-09-3 (paperback)
    Ebook ISBN 978-1-928198-10-9
    1. Romance fiction. 2. Marriage Proposals—Fiction. 3. Blueberry Springs (Imaginary place)—Fiction. 4. Romance fiction

—Small towns. 5. Love stories, Canadian. 6. Small towns—Fiction. 7. Love triangles—Fiction. 8. Interpersonal relations—Fiction. I. Title.

Summary: Three short stories of romance set on Valentine's Day in the fictional small town of Blueberry Springs. Stories of marriage proposals, love triangles, and crushes on best friends.

First Oram Productions Edition: May 2015

ACKNOWLEDGMENTS

Writing a book is not a one-person adventure and I turn to others for assistance with critiquing my story lines, editing, proofreading, and more. To my ladies who make my work all it can be—thank you!

Special thanks also goes to Evelyn Adams, author extraordinaire for *not* voting for the title ideas I had for this boxed set and for pulling the title 'Sweet Treats' out of thin air. Thanks, girl! As well, thank you to my Jeansters for not letting me fall back on a lesser title and for voting for the one that fit best—Evelyn's. XO

Another shout out to my Jeansters—this one goes to (new author) Anne Welch who suggested Adele's *Make Your Feel My Love* as Amber and Russells' song. My Jeansters came up with tons of great song ideas as usual—thank you! I love hanging out with you.

Sweet Treats

I

—————

TEQUILA AND CANDY HEARTS

TEQUILA AND CANDY HEARTS

Okay, so Nicola Samuels may have mentioned her well-known aunts, Mary Alice and Liz, once or twice during the job interview to ensure she was chosen for the position of Blueberry Springs's new community planner. And now that she had the job, all she had to do was bring the flare and gusto she'd promised so she wouldn't receive a pink slip at the end of her probationary period.

Easy, right? Well, maybe if the town wasn't so incredibly boring in the middle of the winter. Nothing thrilling had come across her desk other than the odd building permit, and her will to get out of bed each morning was waning with alarming speed. She'd wanted to grow up and get a real career not realizing it would suck this much.

She needed something exciting. She needed to wake up the small town of Blueberry Springs and put her mark on it. Either that or find a boyfriend. Or even just a best friend who wasn't living his own new life hours away from her. She missed Todd Haber. She hadn't quite realized how close they'd become over the years. Sure, they were best friends who'd barely been apart since high school where they'd shared study notes and a love of

3

all things candy related. When they'd moved on to college they'd shared classes and a cramped old apartment over a Mexican restaurant that had ten different kinds of tequila. After graduation they'd traveled the world, side by side, for two years. But now they were living more than two hours away from each other and she missed him. Needed a friend who understood her and would allow her to bounce crazy ideas off of, someone to get silly over tequila shots and who would play ridiculous card games until the wee hours of the night. But he was in the city and she was here. The middle of nowhere.

Nicola sat back in her cubicle and stared across the open office and through the large windows, wishing she was outside. Fat flakes of snow wandered through the sky, gravity not giving up on its goal of pushing them down to the ground.

Nicola sighed and turned back to the stack of building permits waiting to be checked against local bylaws. She needed to meet new people and fill the hole Todd couldn't from so far away. But where could she meet people? A few weeks ago, she'd borrowed equipment to go cross-country skiing, hoping to find other like-minded souls out on the trails, and had met Jen Kulak, a local nature guide. When she'd asked where everyone their age hung out, Jen had shrugged unhelpfully and said there were a ton of young, single people moving to town these days.

Nicola turned back to her computer, her attention drifting to the photos pinned to the back of her cubicle. One of her doing tequila shots while arm in arm with Todd for a Mexican night she'd organized as president of the college travel club. Her and Todd hiking Mount Fuji. Todd up a coconut tree in the South Pacific. Her learning to surf in Australia. She'd had years of adventure and now she was here. Bored. She had the power to influence the sleepy mountain town, but was at a loss on how to go about doing so.

Tucking her long bob behind her ears, she flipped her desk calendar ahead, checking for holidays she could somehow turn into a community celebration. The only upcoming options were St. Patrick's Day and the spring equinox. Something niggled at the back of her mind and she flicked back to February.

Three and a half weeks until Valentine's Day.

A town full of single people.

Slipping into her parka she tore down the building's front steps, heading to Brew Babies for lunch and reconnaissance. Head down, so she could work through the ideas running through her mind without distraction, she hurried through the cold mountain air, snowflakes sticking to her bangs. Relishing the way the brisk walk perked her up, she hurried into the dimly lit pub and waited for her eyes to adjust to the change in light.

She found the woman she was looking for leaning against her boyfriend as she worked her way through one of Moe's special onion ring double burgers. Which meant it was Friday. Finally. Talk about the slowest week ever. Tomorrow she could drive to the city and hang out with Todd in person rather than video chatting her evening away.

"Hey," Nicola said, feeling more perky as she climbed onto a barstool beside Jen. "How's the special?"

"Good," the woman replied through a mouth thick with food. "Onion ring is perfect and thick."

Jen's boyfriend leaned across her to say, "Like our waists will be if we keep eating this every Friday."

Jen shoved him with her elbow. "We're active. I'm sure we'll survive."

"Hey," Nicola said, before the two went off on a tangent about their latest outdoor adventure. "Did I hear you say that Blueberry Springs's single population has increased? The latest census info isn't available yet."

"Yeah. That's what everyone's saying." Jen wiped her hands on a napkin. "The town is totally appealing to the granola types who want to telecommute from a beautiful mountain. Works for me and my side business. Speaking of which, I'm planning an equipment swap meet at Wally's Sporting Goods. Do you have some things you want to swap?"

"Handbags? An optimistically chosen pencil skirt thinking someday I won't be pear-shaped?"

"Sporting goods."

"Oh, um, no. Sorry. So, how many single people do you think there are in the area?"

Jen shrugged. "Lots. Why?"

"I have an idea." She pushed away from the bar, forgetting about lunch. She didn't have time to waste if she wanted to make a splash.

BACK AT HER DESK, Nicola phoned her aunts, Mary Alice and Liz, who assured her that there were plenty of single people in Blueberry Springs. Which meant there should be enough people seeking someone special—or were at least open to the idea—and could help make her idea fly.

Hanging up the phone, she tapped her pen against a blank notepad, working through various ideas and possibilities. She had less than a month to pull something together for Valentine's Day. During college she'd planned tons of events, but nothing as complex as she wanted to do for Blueberry Springs. She wasn't entirely sure what the town could offer in terms of support, but she was related to two of the most connected women in town and they could—and would—tell her everything she needed to know. Ticket sales could cover the event's costs. A romance-themed trade show could draw both couples and singles. Add in speed dating, outdoor activities such as skating and fireworks, as well as a few competitions and an evening dance, and the day was pretty much planned.

She rolled her chair into the aisle between the cubicles,

stopping beside Don who approved permits and was sometimes good for bouncing ideas.

"Can I get a permit for an event?" she asked.

"Sure." His blue eyes remained focused on the screen in front of him, his reading glasses perched on the end of his short nose. "You know, the secretary used to input all this stuff for me. Before computers revolutionized the work week." His voice held a hint of irony as he backspaced carefully, peering at the screen, then hunted and pecked his way through a correction.

"I want to hold a singles event." Nicola held her breath, waiting for his reaction.

"Good. You could make due with a date since all you talk about is that just-friends guy you're obviously hung up on."

Nicola rolled her eyes. Everyone was getting totally the wrong impression about Todd. Namely, that she was in love him and had been secretly hoping he would come sweep her off her feet.

As if.

They were both happy doing their own thing. Independent and free. And anyway, they'd always had an unspoken agreement that they would be dead honest with each other and never hold anything back about their lives. They could safely flirt and make innuendos but there would never-ever be any perceived intention behind the words or actions. They were just friends and would never complicate things by putting their friendship at risk.

Nicola pushed away the pang of loneliness she felt whenever she thought about Todd these days and focused back on Don and the conversation. "I need a big prize to draw people in."

"Good idea." More hunting and pecking at the keyboard. Finally, he pushed back in his chair and swept his reading glasses onto the top of his head. "Ask businesses for donations."

"Okay, I will. I was also thinking something like five hundred dollars for the winning couple." She tapped her chin in thought.

She was going to need to expand her audience so the thing didn't flop if singles weren't interested in the event. "I'm going to need some events to draw couples in, too."

"In case you and that guy hook up. Smart."

"Very funny."

"What do the couples have to do in order to win?"

She thought fast, discarding ideas until one tickled her fancy. "Engaged. The couple that gets engaged. A bonus if they just met each other!" She clapped her hands, pleased with the idea. Even if nobody got engaged, it would be a talking point for the gossipy little town and possibly draw a few curious onlookers to come out and join the fun. "Is that too cheesy? I can't tell if it is or not."

He scratched the back of his neck, then took a sip of coffee from a reindeer mug. Finally he nodded in approval. "It's okay."

"Don't let Jill see you with that thing." She pretended to shield the cup from anyone walking by. "She finally got all the Christmas stuff put away and has been blowing a hissy fit whenever anyone finds something she forgot." Nicola laughed. "I think the poor gal is contemplating going back to managing the diner."

"When are you having this thing?" Don asked, placing the empty cup on the other side of his monitor so it wouldn't be visible to anyone passing by.

"Valentine's Day."

"*This* Valentine's Day?"

"Yeah."

"You know you won't get overtime for organizing this. And it's not a paid holiday."

She tucked her hair behind her ears, feeling nervous about pulling off an event of this magnitude. "I don't mind working extra." It would get her mind off how lonely she was and how much she was craving adventure.

"What if nobody comes?"

She hadn't thought of that. She paused to think for a moment, then said, "There's nothing better for single people to do in Blueberry Springs on Valentine's Day. Hence me wanting to work extra." She gave him a wink.

Although, come to think of it, she wasn't sure a Valentine's Day event would be something she'd go to—at least not willingly. She hated it when people said *Happy Valentine's Day!* to her, assuming she had someone to share it with other than her goldfish or best friend. The last time she'd had a boyfriend over Valentine's Day before she and Todd became close somewhere around eighth grade.

"Do you think something like this could break even—even if I try to draw in both couples and singles?" she asked, doubts beginning to dance across the forefront of her mind.

Don, who had turned back to his computer and lowered his glasses once again. "Whatever you want, Nicola."

"I just want people to be happy."

"Maybe someone for you finally?" He peered at her over his glasses, his pale blue eyes full of mischief.

She shifted uncomfortably. "It's okay to be single in a small town, you know."

"I'm sure your aunts will find you someone if that Todd fellow doesn't come through."

Unless they found someone like him—fun and easy to hang out with, and looking into the future in the same way she was— she wasn't interested. Which was a good part of why she was single. A man like Todd was rare and she very much doubted someone like that was hanging out in Blueberry Springs just waiting for her aunts to make an introduction.

THAT AFTERNOON, Richard, the man in charge of the Blueberry Springs community center, showed her around the hall. It mostly involved him pointing and grunting at various things and she was starting to wonder if the man spoke English.

"Think anyone will come?" he asked finally.

Ha! He *did* speak English.

"You tell me." She gave him a coy look. "You're single."

The middle-aged man adjusted his ball cap low over his forehead. "Your aunt coming?"

"Liz?" she guessed, seeing as her other aunt, Mary Alice, was married. "Of course. Did you know she likes daisies?"

"Her painted daisies are from my garden."

"You garden?" she asked. "Really?"

"Yep."

A man of few words. Perfect for her aunt who was a big gossip and always had a ton to say. Liz could talk, Richard could listen.

"I'd like to book February fourteenth," Nicola said.

"Put it on the town's account?"

"Yes, please." Everyone in Blueberry Springs knew who she was already, which was an odd feeling. It reminded her of the Filipino village she and Todd had stayed in for a month. As the newcomers, everyone had known who they were and, slowly, they had come to know most of the villagers before they left. Here in Blueberry Springs, her aunts had thrown a party upon her arrival and dragged her through town introducing her to every person they happened across. The few short weeks she'd spent here already felt more like months. She wasn't sure if that was comforting or scary.

"Got that job, did you?" Richard asked.

"I did."

"Know what you're doing?"

"I do."

"Much experience?"

Yeah, nice try, but not going there. "So, how much is it to book this place?"

She received a look that suggested that the man she'd beaten out for the job would have known the answer to that. "Free. It's town property."

"Fantastic. Can I get it the day before to set things up?"

He shook his head. "Bingo night."

"The thirteenth?"

He nodded. "Every Friday."

"Can they move it?"

Judging from Richard's expression, that would be a no. He lightly bounced the building keys in his hand, watching her.

"Would they be okay with me doing setup and decorating around them?"

How big could bingo be in a teensy little town like this, anyway?

As it turned out, bingo was big. Really big. Every Friday evening all the women her aunts' age gathered at the community center to share immense amounts of gossip and dab bingo cards.

Nicola's eyes skimmed over the rows of tables, setting down the box of decorations for tomorrow's event and took a rough head count. If she could get even half this number to come to her Love Extravaganza she'd break even. She should have held a singles bingo event. That would have been killer.

She texted Todd a photo of the bingo hall and before she had a chance to explain what he was seeing, he texted back.

Wow. I didn't realize things were that bad in Blueberry Springs.

What do you mean? she replied.

I'd better warn Liz that you cheat so you don't get lynched.

She snorted and wished she could give Todd a playful push. She had *not* intentionally cheated by falsely calling, *Bingo!* It had been Todd's fault for swiping her hand away from her card, making her dab some of the wrong numbers. The man was like a big, pesky brother half the time.

It's not my fault you can't lose to a girl, she teased.

Seriously, he replied. *First cheating against the little old women in a Scottish hamlet, and now in your aunts' hometown. Whatever is your world coming to?*

Careful or my travel blog will find a more revealing entry about you in San Francisco.

His reply was instant. *Nothing. Happened.* Then, *And no, I am not laughing about that yet.*

Nicola held in a chuckle. There was nothing more fun in the world than teasing Todd about the time she awoke on a bench in the San Francisco harbor after a night on the town to find him spooning a drag queen one bench over.

So what are you doing tonight? she asked. *It looks like I'm pulling an all-nighter seeing as these ladies don't clear out until 11. Trade show vendors arrive at 7. Event starts at 9. Help?*

Her nerves amplified and she wished Todd was here to … just be. She needed a friend. If she hadn't taken into consideration how much bingo could affect her setup plans, what else hadn't she planned for? If she flubbed up, it was good-bye job.

Sorry. No can do. My new boss is evil.

How can your boss be evil? Today was your first day.

Yeah, and I'm already working late.

Why?

As previously stated: my boss is evil.

Is she female?

Sadly, no.

Good.

She wasn't sure why she typed that, but it felt right. She gave herself a shake. It didn't matter if Todd worked under a female boss, he'd never mix work and pleasure and get himself fired. And honestly? It was time Todd settled down and grew up, too.

Jealous? he asked.

I just know that no woman can resist all that is Todd for too long.

No woman can resist this hunk of manliness—other than you. Have you had your head checked?

She laughed, her anxiety about the event washing away. Leave it to Todd to distract her. She'd chosen her B.F.F. well. A winner of the evening's grand prize of two hundred dollars was announced to groans and clapping.

Oh, I think they're done! Gotta go.

Good luck. Wish I was there to help.

Me, too. XO. Without thinking, she'd sent the hug and kiss, not knowing why as it wasn't her usual style. Breath held, she waited for a reply, worried he'd think she'd stepped over the friend line.

An image of them kissing flooded her mind and she blushed, a sudden heat storming through her body.

His reply popped up on her phone and seeing his *XO* reply did funny things to her heart.

"Nicola?" her Aunt Mary Alice called. The woman had had a malignant lump taken out of her throat weeks ago and lightly held a hand against her neck as though warding off future issues.

Nicola jumped, feeling as though she'd been caught doing something she shouldn't.

Her aunt came over, digging around in her cleavage for something. "Where do you want all these tables?" She whipped out one of Nicola's event flyers and scanned it. "Trade show first, right?"

"She wants them in rows," Aunt Liz said, coming over and nudging her sister out of the way.

"Rows would be great," Nicola confirmed. She paused to envision the day. It would start in here with a small trade show which would be followed by a dance in the evening. Speed dating and the other events would be spread around town. She was going to have to be in a million places at once in the afternoon, but it would be worth it. Hopefully.

Mary Alice began telling the bingo women how they could

help with set up as they packed up their bingo dabbers and lucky charms. Acting as a go-between, Nicola's aunt directed the women from setting up the trade fair booths to hanging streamers and red balloons.

Before long the room was set up and Nicola stood back, dazed at how quickly it had all come together. A woman could get used to a town like this.

"Is this extravaganza so you can finally get your hands on that friend of yours Liz keeps telling us about?" asked Wanda, the woman who owned the local wedding store.

"Looking for another customer?" Liz joked.

"He's working tomorrow and we're just friends," Nicola said, surprising herself by wishing on both accounts that he wasn't.

IT WASN'T until after the trade show was well underway the next day that Nicola had a chance to pause, take a breath, and watch the town go by while sipping a cup of coffee.

So far, so good.

Jen had booked a booth to promote her guided hikes and snowshoe tours, and she'd already sold quite a few two-for-one couples deals. She and a few other vendors were already asking if Nicola planned on holding the event again next year. Seeing as it didn't appear she'd ever have anything better to do on Valentine's Day, she'd given an optimistic yes.

Trey, a local teen, had been working the ticket booth and was doing an amazing job. At first, Nicola hadn't been sure about him offering deals if people referred their friends, but when he soon had the place packed, she'd offered him an extra five bucks an hour if he could get them up to fire code. Apparently that hadn't been much of a challenge and people were now waiting to get in.

Nicola savored the moment, the success, and the much-needed caffeine. If only Todd were here to share this with her.

She was going to be talking his ear off via video chat when she finally crawled out of bed tomorrow morning.

"Nicola!" A sweet piece of hunk stopped beside her, his name tag bearing a red rose sticker which indicated he was seeking a relationship. A yellow rose meant seeking friendship and a pink rose meant already taken. Nicola had chosen a yellow rose, but that hadn't stopped several men from asking for her number anyway, claiming that even friends should be able to call each other.

Smart little monkeys.

She read his tag. "Devon Mattson. Any relation to Mandy and her amazing brownies at the Wrap It Up?"

"She's my kid sister. She wanted to know how you wanted the tables for speed dating this afternoon."

"Whatever's easiest," Nicola replied.

He angled closer and she narrowed her eyes. He leaned in with a smile, resting a hand on the wall behind her shoulder, his focus on her lips. He was a bit of a player, this guy. And right now? He was moving in for the kill. But since he was handsome and the brother of her primary brownie source, she didn't shut him down.

"I heard the couple who gets engaged today gets five hundred hot ones," he said.

"True."

Devon dropped down on one knee, pulling a rose from his back pocket.

"Will you marry me, Nicola?"

"You don't even know my last name."

Around them people were turning, watching, and her cheeks flamed.

"Samuels. Marry me, Nicola."

Onlookers chanted, *Say yes!*

Funny. Real funny.

"Devon, don't be ridiculous." She tried to pull him onto

his feet.

"Mandy says we'd be great together. You're adventurous, love to travel, and have a great sense of humor. Plus, I think you're hot."

She tried not to blush and angled her hips away in case he hadn't noticed she was more pear-shaped than sexy hourglass.

"And I've heard you need stitches every three months, Mr. Daredevil. Not interested. But thanks."

"Marry me."

"I think you could do better."

"Not for five hundred bucks."

A passing man paused, then came closer. "Five hundred bucks for proposing to Nicola?" He was on his left knee in seconds, professing his undying love and devotion. Before long, ten men were in kneeling in front of her, asking her to be their wife. Some men, she noted, weren't sure what her name was.

"Up." This was like a romantic comedy that had gotten out of control. Fun, but not the way she wanted to make a splash on the town. "I'm not marrying any of you."

Devon started a new line of pleas, his posse following suit. She couldn't help but chuckle while trying to convince the men to go away. Looking out at the crowd that had gathered, she found a familiar set of eyes watching her with undisguised amusement. The roar of the audience and scattered proposals faded from her mind as the crowd parted to allow Todd through. It was like in a movie. All she needed was for him to sweep her into his arms and kiss her.

She clenched her trembling hands together, trying to play it cool. She reminded herself that they weren't in love. It was just all the Valentine's Day preparations getting to her. He was her best *friend*. Nothing more.

"Don't pick him, pick me!" protested one of the men.

Todd paused by her side, looking confused. "Anything to get

out of marrying me at thirty, huh? You know you still have a few years on the clock."

"You're marrying him? He's not even a local." A man with grey temples smacked his hat against his knee in disgust, weaving his way out of the crowd of impromptu suitors.

"I'm not marrying anyone today," Nicola informed the men, who groaned. "It would hardly be fair for me to win the prize since I'm running the contest, don't you think?" she told the departing men. Devon eyed Todd with interest, the drifting onlookers flowing around him as he remained in place.

"You're marrying people off for money?" Todd whispered, dropping a bag of candy hearts into her palm.

"It's a long story." She glanced at the goody bag. "Oh, fun! You found the X-rated message candies." Nicola threw her arms around him, inhaling his familiar scent, her heart skittering at how right his body felt against hers.

"You know I love long stories," he said when she released him.

"It's not that long. I thought you had to work today?"

"I convinced my boss to allow me to work tomorrow instead."

"Way to go, Nicola!" Liz said, joining them. "I reckon that was at least seventeen proposals. Although Astor is already married so he doesn't count." The woman wrapped Todd in her arms. "Aren't you as dreamy as ever? How about you propose to my Nicola? She's getting old and needs to get married before her best-before date comes up."

"Auntie Liz," Nicola warned.

"I'll do my best," Todd said, "but she's kind of fussy. She wants a house, a dog, and a thriving career before we get married and have fifteen kids. And you know, I'm a rolling stone, Lizzie."

Liz smiled. "Are you sure you could handle her? I finally managed to pin her into one job and look at the commotion she's already caused."

Todd gave Nicola's arm an affectionate squeeze. "She's something all right, isn't she?"

Nicola tugged her friend away from Liz. "I'm borrowing Todd for awhile."

"Hotel above the bar has Valentine's Day special on. You can rent by the hour," her aunt said, eliciting a chuckle from Todd.

Nicola shook her head, cheeks flushing. The woman was incorrigible. And giving her awful ideas about how she could go from friends to lovers with Todd.

As Nicola dragged Todd away from her aunt, he said over his shoulder, "I'll need more than an hour by the time I finally get Nicola to—ow!" He rubbed his shoulder where she'd socked him.

"Don't you give her any more crazy ideas about us. I'll never hear the end of it."

Nicola drew Todd into a nook where she could keep an eye on things while still catching up with her friend. As he told her about his new job her mind kept trying to imagine what it would be like if they took things beyond friendship. The heat of his leg —which was pressed against hers—felt welcoming and inviting. What would he do if she ran her hand up his—stop. Just stop. My word. Her imagination was getting out of hand.

"What's wrong?" he asked, lightly touching her thigh.

She jerked away. "Nothing," she squeaked.

He met her eye, and she was sure he was reading every emotion and every bit of longing she was trying to hide. He stood, swallowing hard, not meeting her gaze again. She could see him drawing the curtain, shutting her out. She'd seen him do it a million times before as women took his friendly openness the wrong way and pushed too close to him.

And now she'd done it herself.

———

Nicola scanned Mandy's crowded restaurant. Speed dating was meant to start in five minutes and the place didn't look particularly ready. It was crammed with people and Mandy was busy trying to serve the crush of people waiting at the café style pick-up counter. Nicola glanced around for Todd, hoping to enlist his help, but he'd stopped at the door to chat with a bombshell who'd commented on his shoes. He was leaning against the doorframe, curving his body closer to the woman so he could presumably be heard over the din of the full restaurant. He was animated, clearly trying to make an impression, holding his right arm out as though climbing an invisible mountain. His climbing Mount Logan story. Yeah, yeah, tallest peak in Canada, blah, blah, blah. Could he be any more obvious?

He was supposed to remain single all day so he could help her out. In other words, be a good best friend and work his butt off alongside her. Not assume she was going to act on whatever he's seen in her eyes a few hours ago and hook up with someone else in order to set her straight on where they stood.

"What do you think?" Mandy asked, joining her. She was looking amazing as ever in a red dress that angled above the knee and gorgeous boots she obviously hadn't purchased anywhere near Blueberry Springs. Nicola didn't think she looked too shabby herself and ran her hands over the wool dress which she'd chosen specifically for the way it flared out, hiding the major impact her wide hips had on her silhouette's shape.

"Has it been this busy all day?" Nicola asked, taking in Mandy's tired expression.

"Since ten," the woman replied, smiling. "Is that Todd? He's cute."

"Um, yeah." She avoided looking at him from someone else's point of view, knowing she'd notice just how sexy he was. She couldn't wait for this holiday to be over so she could get her brain back.

"Uh, oh. I detect a story in that tone," Mandy sang.

"It's nothing." Nicola gestured to the room. Tables were currently scattered as usual, all of them occupied by people looking either excited or stuffed to the brim with nervous dread.

"We have forty participants. Think we could rearrange your place?"

"Sorry. Devon was supposed to do that for me, but he's been too busy proposing to you all day." Mandy gave her a knowing smile and Nicola rolled her eyes.

"The participants signed in beside their names," Mandy said. "It looks like we might be down a guy." She pulled a list off the counter by the cash register, her fingernail trailing down to the one who hadn't signed in. She looked around the room. "Considering the missing man is married, I think we should get someone else to fill in for him."

"I can do it," Todd offered as he walked by.

"No," Nicola replied quickly.

"Why not?" he asked, his eyes daring her to come up with a good excuse.

"You're not signed up."

"So? Sign me up."

"No."

Todd went to help rearrange tables with a huff.

Yeah, okay so she wasn't very good at hiding the fact that she didn't want every woman in Blueberry Springs drooling over him. There was a twist of jealousy in her gut at the thought of him with someone else. Someone local who would bring him to town, but not to see her.

She really needed to get a grip. It was clear she and Todd were only supposed to be friends. If she wasn't careful, she'd push things past the line where things could get awkward and she'd lose the most important person in her life.

Tucking her hair behind her ears and trying not to feel envious, she watched as Mandy's boyfriend drew her away with his arms around her waist, nuzzling her neck. Nicola had loved being single for the past few years and the way she'd been free to travel with Todd and then move to Blueberry Springs for her new job. If you were committed to someone it meant hard decisions when you wanted to change your life, and often led to limiting your options. She wasn't ready for that. When she found someone, she needed to make sure he was like Todd. A man solid enough to say, *Go! Be free! I'll meet you back here at six.* But if she found someone like Todd it would be like replacing him and she never wanted to do that. In fact, she couldn't even imagine life without him.

Searching the room for Todd, she found him chatting with a different woman who blushed and giggled as they pushed tables into a long row. She knew him well enough to know that he was avoiding her.

Shaking herself out of her thoughts, Nicola blew her heart-shaped whistle to gather everyone's attention.

"If you are signed up for speed dating, sit on this side of the room if you're a guy. Gals on the other. When I blow my whistle at the end of three minutes, guys get up and move one chair to the right. Have fun and see if you can find someone interesting. Exchanging phone numbers is fine. And if you happen to get engaged to someone you meet today, you could win a five hundred dollar gift certificate good at any Blueberry Springs store. So, guys, no pressure."

Chuckles rippled through the room, eyes twinkling at the possibility of love and money being found in the next thirty minutes.

"Any questions?" she asked.

"Nicola?" a man called from the back of the restaurant. "Will you marry me?"

He was cute and buff. Had to be a climber with shoulders like that. She caught another glance at the man.

"Devon Mattson!" she scolded. "I already turned you down today. Several times." He'd ambushed her every time he saw her and she was starting to expect him as well as the adrenalin rush that came with each new proposal. It was harmless fun and unlike with Todd, she knew and remembered her role. Just play along, and don't take the attention seriously. Her gaze flickered to Todd. He was keeping an eye on Devon and she wondered if her friend felt the same sting of unwanted jealousy she did when he attracted the opposite sex.

Man, she'd messed up letting the day get to her. She needed to figure out a way to get their friendship back on track again.

"You will be mine, Nicola." Devon winked and grinned, taking a seat across from a rather intimidated looking woman at the end of the line. He reached across the table to shake her hand. "I'm Devon, single and devastatingly handsome in case those glasses of yours are dirty."

"Please take your seats." Nicola placed the whistle to her lips and raised a stopwatch.

"We're short a woman," Mandy pointed out.

"What? I thought we were short a man?"

Jen joined them, her nose ring twinkling under the overhead lights. She quickly counting the participants. "Yup. Short a woman."

Todd had taken a seat in the lineup, still chatting with the woman he'd introduced himself to. He was pouring on the charm, but Nicola noticed he was already beginning to withdraw as he often did when the women got too interested. He'd liked to chase, but not catch.

"Todd?" Nicola asked, "Could you step out so we're even?"

"I think you should step in," he said, with a grin wicked enough to rival Devon's.

What kind of twisted game was he playing?

"Then who will run the stopwatch?"

"I will," Jen said. "Mandy has to run the cash register. She has customers." She tugged the stopwatch and whistle from Nicola. "In you go."

Nicola gave a dramatic sigh to the group who cheered her on. "Fine, fine," she muttered. What was there to lose? She may as well jump in, if only to see what needed to be worked on for next year's event. As well as find out what Todd was up to.

She took a seat at the end, across from a man old enough to be her grandfather. Jen blew the whistle. The man stared at her and smacked his gums. He seemed to have forgotten his false teeth.

Why had she chosen three minutes? Why not, say … one?

"Hi, I'm Nicola."

"Reggie. I'm spoken for, but I'm keeping my options open."

"And how's that going for you?"

"Well …" He paused to consider her question. A gray-haired woman tottered over and yanked him up by the ear. Gran. Beth Wilkinson's grandmother.

"What in tarnation's name do you think you are doing, Reggie Max?"

Gran yanked on the sleeve of a man standing nearby and plunked him at the table in Reggie's place, berating her boyfriend as she hauled him out into the crisp February afternoon.

Laughing, Nicola didn't get a chance to introduce herself to the new recruit before Jen blew the whistle again and a man a little closer to her age took the seat opposite.

"My wife sent me," he said.

What was it with married men and speed dating? Was Blueberry Springs a hotbed of extramarital affairs? If it was, she was sure she would have gotten fair warning from her aunts.

"She wanted me to see what a good catch she was," said the man.

Well, this event was going downhill so fast she didn't know whether to ride it out with a thrilled scream, or to bury her face in agony and horror.

Several long minutes later, Jen blew the whistle again and Nicola was faced with another man. As the half hour wore on, her prospects gradually got better. She even got a few phone numbers. When she looked down the line, she caught Todd's eye. He gave a small smile and nod. Things were okay again.

Thank goodness.

Then came Devon. "Nicola, will you marry me?"

"No."

"Jen, blow the whistle, please?"

Jen shook her head with false remorse. "Sorry, still two and a half minutes to go. Devon, tell her about your dog or your marathons or something."

"Why do you want that prize so bad?" Nicola asked, before he repeated the things her aunts had already listed off while going through the town's most eligible men roster they kept perpetually updated in their memory banks.

"Five hundred dollars could buy a lot of new climbing equipment at Wally's. Well, two-fifty since I'd split it with you." He gave her a warm grin.

Gran slipped by, whispering in Nicola's ear, "If you ever mistake lust for love, there's always divorce. I recommend going through several husbands until you find exactly the right one."

"So romantic," Nicola said dryly. "Where's Reggie?"

"He needed a nap so I'm back to scope out my options. Just in case." She smiled and tottered away to ask Mandy if she had any sherry.

"Is that a no?" Devon asked.

Nicola sighed. "Still a no."

"Say that five times fast." He leaned on his hands, watching her expectantly.

She laughed as Jen blew the whistle.

And then there was the man she hadn't realized she'd been waiting for. Todd. The last man in line.

"Hi," she put on a sultry voice, suddenly tired of her stupid event and uncertain of how to act in front of Todd without him taking things the wrong way. Best to play the goof. "What's your name, big boy?"

He placed his strong forearms on the table and leaned closer. "I already like the sound of where you're going with this small talk."

"Odd and interesting name. Quite long as well. Do you have a nickname? Or shall I just call you Big Boy?"

She got a mischievous grin that relaxed her. "Any hobbies?" he asked.

"Anything my best friend Todd wants to do."

He broke eye contact, shifting away, chest tight with what appeared to be a pent up breath. "You really need to stop using that voice."

Nicola sat straighter, feeling embarrassed. "Why?"

"Because it's doing strange things to my mind and I might mistake my best friend for a girlfriend."

And would that be so bad? a small voice in the back of her mind asked.

"You have one of those?"

"No. Not yet."

"Yet?"

"I've taken myself off the market." He cupped his hands over hers. His eyes were quiet, his face battling a variety of emotions as though he was caught between wanting to withdraw and wanting to get closer.

"Why?" she whispered, leaning in, heart racing.

The whistle blew and she flinched. Todd slid his hands back onto the table and Jen whisked her away to set up the next round of speed dating before she could figure out what Todd was up to and what it meant to their friendship.

THE DANCE HAD STARTED, the whole day a definite success. Nicola propped herself against the wall in the community center's lobby and took a long, slow breath, waiting for Todd to join her after he finished returning a call to his dad. A few more hours to go, then she could go home and massage her aching feet.

"Congratulations," her boss said, giving her a pleased smile. "You've done an amazing job."

"Thanks. We've even made a profit."

"People are happy and so am I. Take the rest of the night off," he said with a wink, heading into the dance.

She wished she could call it a day, but she still had to pay the DJ and close up after everyone left. The very idea of staying on her feet for another four hours caused her to yawn. At least it looked as though she didn't have to worry about whether she'd be kept on as Blueberry Springs's community planner.

New couples came in from the cold, holding hands or chatting, heads tipped together in conversation.

The man she'd hired to come dressed as Cupid flitted through the lobby, pretending to shoot people with his plastic bow. People laughed and Nicola watched as he broke the ice between nervous singles, giving them something to talk about. Cupid was going on the do-again list for next year.

Stepping into the dance hall, Nicola hugged herself, watching as Trey asked a fellow high school cutie to dance. Nicola had ensured she talked about how awesome he'd been all day within the gal's earshot after she noticed how he'd kept glancing over at the girl. The young couple joined others on the dance floor, moving behind Officer Malone who was looking resplendent in full uniform and dancing with his friend Amber. That woman seemed completely clueless about how much the man was gaga for her and Nicola wondered if it was because Amber was living with someone. Then again, not everyone got their happily ever after when it came to love. Kind of like her.

Nicola turned, feeling someone standing close.

"May I have this dance?" Todd gave a regal bow, hand extended.

"Just don't propose. I've had enough of those for the day."

"My dad was asking about you."

"The fact that you mention this on the heels of proposal talk worries me," she joked, feeling inexplicably nervous.

Todd gripped her waist, ballroom dancing them through the crowd which was jumping to a rap song.

"Yeah, he told me to make an honest woman of you, but I'll have to tell him you said no."

"Next time, bring a ring."

"What makes you think I don't have a ring?"

She stared him in the eye. He was messing with her and his seriousness faked. It had to be. There was no way he was thinking about taking the friends-to-lovers leap. Even after the uncertain hand-holding during speed dating.

"I've missed you," he said, drawing her closer. The heat from his body warmed her and she looked up into his familiar dark gaze. So many memories. So many good times as friends.

"I've missed you, too, Todd."

Without thinking, she curled up onto her tip toes and gently kissed his lips. She pulled back, her heart pounding, confused about how much she wanted *this*.

The look in Todd's eyes went from affection to a hint of shock and surprise as well as something she couldn't quite decipher. Something that looked a lot like him pulling that curtain across, blocking her out. Panic coursed through her and she broke free of his loose hold.

They were friends. Only friends. She'd stormed across an unspoken line, broken the contract. He didn't want this. He wasn't looking for a girlfriend. She was supposed to be the one woman he could joke and flirt with without her taking it the wrong way, and now she'd ruined it.

"I'm sorry. That was a mistake. All of this Valentine's Day stuff got to me for a second. I only want to be friends," she said quickly, waving her hands and giving a nervous laugh as she turned away, hoping the crowd would swallow her up. "I … have to go help the DJ. Good night."

She heard Todd call to her as the dancers swept her away, but she didn't turn back, afraid of what she'd find in her best friend's eyes, and fearful of how much it would hurt to see.

She had been stupid, kissing him. If they tried being lovers and didn't make it, she wouldn't just lose a boyfriend, she'd lose everything. The very thought scared her so badly, she had trouble breathing. If given the choice, she'd deny herself love in order to not lose what they had together.

But it wouldn't be easy. In her heart, she knew Todd was the only thing that had ever felt truly right in her life and that she was irreversibly, irrevocably, head over heels in love with him.

Turning, she glanced back, watching as he ran a hand through his hair, slowly sifting his way through the crowd. As though sensing she was watching, he looked over and their eyes met from across the dance floor. A current passed between them and Nicola thought in that moment that maybe he wanted her, too. That things were going to change for them. A couple moved, blocking her view and the connection broke. A moment later, when the path between them cleared, he was gone and Nicola was overcome with the sensation that she'd just lost everything.

The End

II

WHISKEY AND GUMDROP HEARTS

WHISKEY AND GUMDROP HEARTS

 andy Mattson yawned as she placed the day's batch of her national award-winning whiskey and gumdrop brownies into her restaurant's oven. Wiping her hands on her apron, she set about mixing up a quadruple batch for tomorrow. Blueberry Springs's first 'Love Extravaganza' Valentine's Day event would be taking place all over town and in the afternoon her café-style restaurant would be full of speed daters. Meaning she would need extra of pretty much everything that sold well such as her brownies.

Making sure her long blonde hair hadn't escaped the hair net, she leaned down to inhale the bowl's cocoa and butter combination. Nothing smelled as wonderful—other than her boyfriend Frankie Smith. He'd helped her get her restaurant off the ground last year, and while the place was doing really well, the success still didn't feel like her own. She owed too much to too many people—her boyfriend included.

Looking at the bowl of mixed batter she contemplated increasing the batch. More brownies sold meant more money going toward her debts. Sighing, she poured what she had into pans, not having the time nor extra pans to increase the already large batch. Wiping her hands on her apron, she checked on the brownies already in the oven. Ten more minutes to go. There was a light rap at the back door and she swung it open, expecting her brother, Ethan, who helped out in the mornings before going home to build websites in the afternoon. It would be a first having him arrive on time.

"Frankie!" Mandy wrapped her arms around her tall boyfriend, drawing him into the warmth of the kitchen, his arms a strong presence around her. His cheeks were rosy from the cold.

"I brought you something." He placed two insulated cups on the counter and leaned in to give her a long, deep kiss. "I figured you likely hadn't started the coffee maker yet with all you have to do for tomorrow."

"Mmm. You're wonderful." She slid her hands around his neck, his winter coat getting in the way of feeling more skin. "Maybe you should step into my office. I have ten minutes until the next batch of brownies needs attention."

"I'm going to need longer than a few measly minutes, Mandy Mattson." He nibbled on her bottom lip then deepened the kiss, his mittened hands running up her ribs.

"Please?" She removed his mitts and tugged on his coat, trying to pull him toward her office off the kitchen.

"We have to stop meeting like this." He kissed her neck, stopping her from drawing him away. He held her hands in his, leaching their heat. "Move in with me."

At first she thought he was joking, testing the idea as he had several times before, but this time his eyes were serious.

She took a step back, smoothing the front of his jacket. If she moved in with him she'd never make it in for her early morning baking sessions. Right now she lived across the street from Frankie's grandfather's old building where her restaurant was housed which meant she could roll out of bed any hour to get work done. If she lived with Frankie she'd be too tempted to stay snuggled against his warmth, particularly on cold, black mornings such as today and she needed to stay on top of her business if she expected to be able to expand it as planned.

"I need to see you more," Frankie said. "I miss you."

"I'm right here." She turned away, running a damp cloth over the counter. She needed to finish up the brownies, resterilize the counter, then prep and package breakfast sandwiches for the morning crowd.

"No, you're always flitting about, hurrying from one thing to the next."

"Frankie, it's—"

"I know. This business is your passion and the first years are important, but you're going to burn out."

"I'm fine." Stifling a yawn, she tossed him the bag of gumdrop hearts that would go on top of tomorrow's brownies, hoping he'd let the subject drop. "Help yourself."

He set the unopened bag on the counter. "You're exhausted."

"There's a lot going on tomorrow. And anyway, it's worth a few late nights and early mornings if it gets my loans paid off early. I'm *so* close to getting through the last of the micro loans already." Then she'd feel successful. Then she'd be able to be an equal in her partnership with Frankie instead of always the one in need.

"And then will you chill out and enjoy what you have?"

She ignored his question.

"You still want to open a second place, don't you?" He crossed his arms over his chest as he studied her. "Is this about more income? Because making more work for yourself won't make you rich."

"I'm not looking to get rich, just pay off my debts." She struggled under the intensity of his gaze as she placed her baking bowls in the dishwasher. "If I expand, in five years I'll be way ahead of the game."

"Why can't the success of this place be enough?"

"I just … it sounds silly but I need to prove that I can do this."

"You already have." Anger was starting to edge his voice.

"Frankie, it feels like everything was given to me. The micro loans, the building—"

"You're paying rent on this place. You're paying back the loans. You're in here every day of the week killing yourself. Your brownies won a national baking competition. People come here because they love your food, your place, your service. They don't have to be loyal to you. We're a nice town, but not that nice. This success is yours. It's time you owned it."

Mandy brushed off his kind words as tears pricked her eyes. It wasn't just the need for success that kept her working so hard, but how could she explain the real reason to Frankie?

She pulled the first batch of brownies out of the oven, then loaded in tomorrow's extra batch. Frankie fell silent as she worked and she became immersed, moving on to the next step in her morning routine.

"I've waited half my life for you," he said quietly.

She paused to look at him, hands still in the bin of lettuce she was washing.

With hands flat on the island, eyes level with hers, Frankie said, "If you expand, you're telling me to wait at least another five years before I'll ever truly have you in my life."

Her breath caught in her throat. "I'm in your life."

"Do you really actually love me, Mandy?"

"What kind of question is that? You know I do."

They stared at each other for a moment.

Frankie fidgeted with the bag of gumdrops. "Sometimes I feel as though you use this place as a way of avoiding me."

Mandy's throat tightened. She loved Frankie with all her heart and had since they were teens. It had been a big step allowing herself to finally trust in their love. She'd turned her best friend into a lover and he'd been a huge part of helping her make her dream of running her own restaurant come true. How could he ever doubt how much she cared?

She bit her lip and focused on rinsing the lettuce, fighting back the pain in her chest. She needed to push hard to make her restaurant as profitable as she could, needed to expand. Why didn't he see that? She needed it so she could be with him. Because if she moved in with him, then a proposal would come. That meant a wedding. She couldn't afford a wedding, and her family sure as heck wouldn't be paying for one. Frankie was doing okay with his car restoring business, but it wouldn't be fair to have him pay for their entire wedding—especially when he wanted to build a bigger shop and move to doing the work full-time. Not when he'd already done so much to help her get to where she was now. It was her turn to pull some weight.

"Move in with me," he said again. "I miss you. We can spend more time together. I won't be rushing home in the mornings to let Heart outside. You won't be hurrying home to feed Portia."

"You think my cat and your dog will get along under one roof?" she joked, trying to deflect the conversation.

"We can move into my place. There's plenty of room."

His place was tiny, but she knew she'd fit right into the space, loving how she'd be tucked tight against her man.

"I'll think about it," she said, finally.

"What's there to think about?"

"I can't afford it."

"Your expenses won't change," he said with infinite patience. "We'll actually end up further ahead because we'll be sharing rent —well, my mortgage."

"So, you're looking for a sugar mama to pay your mortgage?" She gave him a saucy smile, but he remained serious.

"Mandy." He reached over and stilled her working hands. "This isn't how love works. When two people love each other, they spend as much time together as possible. We barely spend more than a few hours a week in the same room, and when we do all we talk about is work. It's not healthy and we need to make some changes."

Change meant losing. Losing income. Losing the chance to be an equal. Losing the chance to make it all back to the man she loved. Losing the chance to help him reach his own dreams.

Mandy, unable to speak, continued to work, head bent low.

***

MANDY SAT IN HER OFFICE, joining the conference call that would determine whether the other Wrap It up chain owners would approve her plans for expansion or not. Crossing her fingers and taking a deep breath, she put a smile in her voice and greeted the other women.

Ethan popped his head through the office door, using one crutch to support himself—not a bad day for her brother who was still recovering from a bad car accident last year. "Hey, are we out of tomatoes?"

She frowned at the disruption and placed a thumb over the speaker on her phone. "Check the crate under the island."

"Already did."

"We can't be out."

"About a dozen got frozen in transit. Forgot to tell you I tossed them."

She was going to have to talk to the trucker about how to handle produce in the winter. "Another shipment comes this afternoon. We'll have to make do until then."

Her brother nodded and went back to the kitchen. She lifted her thumb from the speaker and listened to the ladies chat about their month and a few changes they had in mind for their own restaurants. They'd all banded together when the original franchise owner had tried taking them all for a ride. They'd come out on top in the end, and in the process had become not only business partners but life-long friends that trusted each other implicitly.

"So, Mandy?" Blair Diggs asked. "When are you going to share your award-winning brownie recipe with the rest of the chain?"

Mandy chuckled at the running joke. "I don't know, how are the weather conditions in Hell?"

The women roared with laughter and one of them groaned. "Blueberry Springs is too far to go to get my hands on those things."

"Yeah, but it's better for your figure that way," another replied. "We can't eat too many."

"So," Mandy said, "Did you have a chance to read over my projections? What do you ladies think about me opening another location?" An awkward silence stretched over the line and her stomach fell into a crumpled mess in her pelvic region. "Did you get my proposal?"

"I got it, but I'm just not sure expanding so soon is a good idea," Lexi said. "It was exhausting running two places when I gave it a go. I was worried and stressed all the time."

"Right, but this is a different situation," Mandy said. Lexi's expansion had been fraught with bad luck, bad timing, as well as fudged projections from the old owner. Mandy had checked all the angles and done the math several times over. She knew it could work—all she needed was the approval of her fellow brand owners.

"Mandy, I just don't think the timing is right. It's too financially risky." It was Diana, the owner of the flagship restaurant. "You're just getting your feet under you. Opening a second place may sound like a good idea, but it's going to spread you too thin. You're not going to be able to physically keep up with the demand of two places."

"How many hours a week are you spending in your restaurant right now?" Blair asked.

What a question. It was easier to work out how many hours she *wasn't* spending here.

"If you haven't hired a manager," Blair continued, "and don't feel safe leaving it for a one week vacation, then you aren't ready to expand."

Vacation? What was that?

"I can leave this place for a few days." She was sure of it. Although her best employee—her brother—wasn't exactly the most reliable person. She'd considered hiring a manager, but wasn't really sure what she'd do with her time if someone else was managing things. Managing was *her* job. Plus, paying another employee would interfere with paying down her debts as fast as possible.

"I need to think about it a bit more," Blair said.

The others quickly agreed and Mandy breathed a sigh of relief. Her plan was still a possibility.

"You need to think about how expansion would affect your everyday life as well, Mandy," Blair said. "Talk to everyone tomorrow?"

They all agreed on a time and hung up.

Mandy stared at the silent phone, feeling defeated. She made her way into the restaurant to prepare for the lunch crowd, her heart not in it. She was sure she didn't have to be here every day, she just chose to be. Why couldn't the women see that?

Standing behind the pick-up counter, she wondered if Frankie would come by for his usual soup and sandwich. He'd been pretty hurt when he'd left that morning.

Smiling, she served her regular customers, loving the way her place was filling up with her regulars as well as a few new faces.

"Mandy Mattson?" a man asked, butting into line.

"The line starts back there," she replied, pointing.

"Actually I was hoping to speak to you. I'm Theodore Chase with the Hungry Man grocery chain. I'd like to chat about the possibility of our two companies working together."

"I already have my suppliers, but if you have a price list I don't mind taking a look." She handed the customer she'd been serving his change and called the next person in line.

"Actually, we were wondering about your brownies. The ones that won nationals." He indicated a stack of brownies under the glass dome to his right. "The whiskey and gumdrop ones."

"You've tried them?" She didn't remember seeing him in here before.

"Love them. We'd like to carry them in our store."

"Ethan? Can you take over?" Mandy asked, leading Theodore through the kitchen and into her small office, barely daring to breathe at the possibility of a new deal. "Sorry, there's not a lot of room in here."

The man took the chair wedged between the door and her desk. "Basically, we'd like to try once a week shipments," he said, smoothing his thinning hair over his crown. "We have forty successful stores across the country and would like to try selling your brownies in three local outlets. A three month trial."

"How many brownies per week for each store?" She held her breath, hoping for a big number.

"Forty half dozen packages. Per week, per store to start."

She was going to need a better cocoa supplier. And possibly cheaper butter in order to boost her profits. And more ovens. A lot more.

There went any profits.

"Don't your stores have their own bakeries?" she asked, considering her competition.

"Yes, but we would stop making brownies for the duration of your contract. You'd be our exclusive brownie supplier."

"Why?"

"Because we've tried yours. And honestly, we've tried replicating the recipe and can't figure it out. Yours also have a blue ribbon. Why not deliver the best to our customers?"

She sat back, stunned. This could be huge.

"Will you buy them outright or am I on the hook for expired goods?"

"It's all in the contract." He began rifling through his briefcase. "You would be responsible for your own packaging, delivery. Bring them to us ready to sell."

Mandy looked at the spreadsheets he laid in front of her as well as the offer. If packaging and delivery didn't cost too much, she could make a tidy profit—solving some of her money worries. The problem was, she'd need a bigger kitchen which wouldn't come cheap.

"When do you need to know by?"

"The offer is good until the end of the month."

If she could swing a way to produce that many brownies in a short window of time each week, she might be able to really get things moving in her life as well as marry her best friend before he got tired of waiting.

Maybe.

———

MANDY LET herself into Frankie's house, scratching his big dog, Heart, behind the ears as she sought out her boyfriend.

"Frankie?" she called. "Guess what?"

"I'm in the kitchen."

"That is a total turn-on by the way. Being in the kitchen."

"Too bad for you I'm wearing clothes."

She leaned against the doorway. "That can easily be remedied."

"You big tease. I know as soon as I get some food in you you're going to crash on the couch."

"You're probably right." Stretching, Mandy let out a yawn. "I'm bagged, and tomorrow's going to be crazy busy."

Frankie handed her a plate of his homemade mac 'n' cheese from the microwave.

"Thanks." She sat at the table. "Did you already eat?"

He nodded.

She dug into the food, happy it was something different than the sandwiches she usually ate at her restaurant. "Mmm. Comfort food. I needed this." Trying to tell herself she wasn't disappointed that Frankie had already eaten—it was after nine at night, so of course he'd eaten—she bolted down her meal. She needed to make some changes in regards to her eating habits. She ate too late, then ate too much, too fast. Since opening her place she'd gained five pounds, despite being run off her feet every day.

"What was I supposed to guess?" Frankie asked, joining her at the table. She loved this part of her day. It didn't happen often, but sometimes she managed to sneak away from work before he turned in. Tomorrow was going to be busy and, technically, she should still be working, but she needed Frankie to know he was a priority. Plus, she wanted to share her latest news.

"Hungry Man asked if I'd supply them with my whiskey and gumdrop brownies."

"Get out of town!" Frankie got up and gave her a massive hug, lifting her out of the chair. But when he let her go again, she could see the worry in his eyes. Which meant they were set for another argument about how hard she worked.

Instead, he sat and said, "That's great news."

"It's a real compliment, but I don't know if I can do it." Mandy pulled her hair out of its ponytail, shaking out her mane. Frankie's eyes darkened with desire and she felt herself blush. She'd never get enough of how he looked at her.

"Of course you can," he said.

"What happened to me working too hard?"

"You looking to fight?" He tugged her hand, pulling her onto his lap. "Maybe there are other ways to get your success without opening another restaurant, Mandy. Something less likely to wear you out."

"It's only a three month contract. The overhead probably

won't even allow me to break even. And if it doesn't work out, I'll have all this extra equipment and nothing to do with it."

"What do you mean?"

"Where am I going to bake over seven hundred brownies in one day? They have to be delivered fresh." And how was she going to make sure her restaurant stayed on track if she was busy working on this? She'd need more staff to fill the hole her absence would create.

"The community center rents out their industrial kitchen. You could bake a ton of brownies in there in a few hours."

"Why didn't I think of that?" She grabbed his chin and pulled him to her for a kiss.

"There's a reason to keep me around, now isn't there?"

"Of course there is."

"Then why don't you move a few things in here with me? I have lots more ideas just waiting for you to ask."

She hesitated.

"I'm serious."

She nodded, unable to face him.

The playful tone in his voice vanished. "Look." He pushed her off his lap so he could stand. "You need to do some serious thinking about you and me and where you want this to go. If we've already run our course as a couple, I need to know now—not after I've spent several more years waiting for you." He walked them to the door, helping her into her coat, avoiding her eyes. "You have a big day tomorrow, get some rest."

Mandy paused in the doorway. "I love you, Frankie."

"Yeah?" He didn't seem thoroughly convinced.

"Yeah." She gave him a long kiss, not wanting to leave. "Always."

"Then you can prove it to me tomorrow when I ask you if you're still serious about us."

MANDY FLEW around her restaurant's kitchen, nearly dropping the platter of special Valentine's Day brownies she was carrying. Her hands had started shaking when Frankie had booted her out of his house last night with his pre-breakup speech and they hadn't stopped since. She'd barely slept a wink and felt as though she was on the verge of tears. She had to choose between her two dreams. Her livelihood or her boyfriend. It shouldn't be this way. They should go hand-in-hand if they were both meant to be, but she knew she couldn't give him all he needed *and* expand.

The restaurant had been decorated for Valentine's Day—nothing major, just streamers and paper hearts—and this afternoon Nicola Samuels, the Love Extravaganza event planner, would be hosting the speed dating competition here. If it went well, Mandy could earn a little extra toward paying off her debts. If it didn't go well …

Sucking in a deep breath, she double-checked her coffee maker to ensure it was still working. Her espresso machine. The expiry date on the cream.

The bell above the door jangled as she wiped the last table from the breakfast rush. Frankie.

He stood in the doorway, watching her in his quiet, patient way and she nervously waited for him to speak.

"Hey," she said finally, walking over to him when he remained silent. Her red dress clung to her body as she moved and she watched Frankie's reaction to her outfit. He was still interested in her and her hands finally stopped shaking. She wanted to hug him and kiss him and never, ever let go, knowing he loved her—loved her so much he was willing to let her go if need be.

"Happy Valentine's Day," she said.

His coat was cold, giving her a chill as he pulled her tight for a hug and a kiss.

He offered her a bouquet that had been bundled in plastic to protect it against the cold. "Will you be mine, Mandy?"

She smiled and kissed his cold lips again. "Always."

"Yeah?" he asked, raising an eyebrow hopefully.

She stiffened. She couldn't afford a wedding—not even a small one. And with their large families and the town feeling as though it was one big extended family, she knew they wouldn't be able to get by with a small service. How would she find the time to plan something like that? Her career needed to get off the ground first. Things needed to be easier.

"I made you something." She turned and reached under the pick-up counter for a special batch of brownies.

He chuckled. "Brownies?"

"There might be a surprise or two involved. See if you can figure them out."

He frowned at the plate and set it down, peeling back the shrink wrap.

Mandy's eldest brother Devon ambled in, shaking the cold out of his coat. "Hey guys." He reached for a brownie and Frankie slapped his hand away as he began rearranging the gumdrop-less squares, lining up the icing stripes until they formed a completed puzzle: be mine.

"Yeah," Frankie said, looking up at Mandy, resolve in his gaze. "Always."

"I'm going to get a coffee from Ethan," Devon said, easing away. "This is getting kind of mushy and private."

"Not yet, man. Not yet," Frankie replied with a grin as he swept Mandy into his arms for a deep, luscious kiss that made her head spin.

"Well, do me a favor and get her knocked up," Devon said when Frankie released her. "I need her and that truck of hers off the meadow's race track so I can win for once."

"Dream on," Mandy said, reaching over to give her brother a shove. "Maybe you should get off the track if you can't keep up with your kid sister."

"I swear Frankie's been giving you tips."

"She pays me well," Frankie said, waggling his eyebrows suggestively.

"Ugh." Mandy gave him a shove as well. "I have work to do. Make yourself at home, but don't eat anything unless you've paid for it." She pointed a finger at her eldest brother.

"What happened to the family discount?" Devon asked, arms out in protest as Frankie disappeared into the kitchen.

"Wah, wah, wah," Mandy said, keeping an eye on Devon. He could go through twenty dollars' worth of brownie profits if left alone for five minutes.

"Ethan?" Frankie called as he returned to the dining area, carrying Mandy's coat. "You got the place?"

Mandy's youngest brother nodded.

"Come on," Frankie said, trying to corral her with her open coat. "We have a challenge to get to."

"I have to work."

"Thanks for reminding me," Devon said, snatching a brownie from Frankie's plate. "I have to go propose to Nicola so I can win five hundred hot ones." He popped the brownie in his mouth and, a moment later, pulled a wax paper wrapped note from his gooey mouth. "What's this?"

Mandy snatched it from him in disgust. Frankie plucked the note from her fingers and carefully unwrapped it. He raised his eyebrows and smiled at Mandy, hugging her close. "Are there more of these?"

"What a way to ruin a perfectly good brownie," Devon said as he exited, heading toward the community center.

"Every piece has a note or a coupon," Mandy said. Last night, she'd decided to give her boyfriend what he wanted—more time. Each brownie promised him a date, a trip to the city, a movie, or something they would do together—away from work.

Frankie kissed her nose and set the plate behind the counter. "Come with me." He held out his hand, her coat in the other.

She acquiesced, letting him lead her out of the restaurant.

"What's the challenge?" Mandy asked, buttoning her coat while wracking her brain for what Nicola had planned for her extravaganza and what Frankie might be dragging her off to. She had a ton to do today and hoped it wouldn't take too long. At the same time, she wasn't about to push him away when he'd made it clear he'd been taking a long, hard look at their relationship lately.

"The Greatest Couple in Blueberry Springs." He pulled her into the community center, paying their admission and pinning a corsage on her dress with care. Red, to show she was taken. "You're mine, Mandy. And we're going to show the town just how good we are together."

"We'll never beat Cynthia and Dan," she said, taking in their competition. "You can't beat them at the newlywed game when they're actually married. Plus, it's their anniversary today."

She couldn't help but wish that she and Frankie were married. It felt like a loss every time she shied away from his hints about moving in together or tying the knot. And lately, the doubt and hurt in his eyes was becoming too much to take. She just needed more time so she could join him as an equal and not as a dependent.

MANDY KISSED Frankie as they headed back to her restaurant. They hadn't won the title of The Greatest Couple in Blueberry Springs, but she'd had an amusing moment watching Devon get shut down as he proposed to Nicola. It was obvious he wasn't going to win the five hundred dollar prize for getting engaged at the extravaganza today.

On stage, she and Frankie had answered questions with ease, and she'd been reminded of all that was good between her and Frankie. They were a good team who had a lot of history, trust, and love. Which meant she really needed to find a way to enjoy what they had. She wanted to move in with him, get married, and live happily ever after.

But how?

Hurrying through her to-do list, she began prepping for the soon-to-arrive lunch crowd and then the speed dating session. The community center had been packed and it was likely to be the same here when people came looking for a meal.

Ethan stopped her as she hurried into the dining area. "Your office phone is ringing."

She hadn't even heard it and she checked the time, realizing it was the conference call she'd been waiting for. It was time for the final decision on expansion and she half hoped they'd say yes, and half hoped they'd say no.

"If I'm not back out in an hour," she told Ethan, "can you make sure this speed dating check in list gets put on the counter and that participants sign it?" She handed him the sheet and went to answer her phone.

"Mandy!" Blair crowed into the phone. "How are ya?"

"Good. Just getting ready for an event. What's the word?" She wiped her sweaty palms on her dress, her heart beating like she was racing around the dirt track against Devon and Frankie.

Silence.

"Hello?"

Blair let out a reluctant sigh and Mandy's heart sunk.

"It's too risky, Mandy. The expansion. The financial risk is just too great. It will overextend you in every way and it takes so much energy. As those who love you, we say it's not time. It doesn't feel right."

"It doesn't feel right?" What kind of business-minded individual used that as an excuse?

"I'm sorry, Mandy. I know you're eager. Maybe in a year."

Diane and Lexi started talking over each other, trying to console her.

"You're not upset, are you?" Blair asked.

Mandy let out a choked laugh. "No, no. Not at all. Just wondering what I'm going to do with all this free time."

The women laughed with her. They knew how hard Mandy worked because, as business owners, they did too.

"What is Frankie doing for you for Valentine's Day?" asked Lexi.

"Frankie?" Her heart dropped and she wondered how she was ever going to be equal enough to stand beside him as a true partner if she didn't expand.

"You two are still together, aren't you?"

"Oh," Blair said, "Don't tell me you're putting that place ahead of that fantastic thing the two of you have going on."

Someone clucked in disappointment.

"No, no. I just forgot for a moment that it was Valentine's Day." She sat quietly, barely daring to breathe as she envisioned her debt-laden future. She should have kept working as a waitress. She should never have tried making this work.

Mandy gave a heavy sigh, and Blair said, "Girls, you can hang up. Mandy and I have things to discuss."

Lexi laughed. "Please don't tell me you're giving her relationship advice?"

"I've learned a lot with all those men and it's time to pass it on. Remember, meeting in Dakota in two weeks, ladies."

The other women hung up and Mandy was tempted to do the same. "It's a busy day here, Blair. Can we do this some other time?"

"Why do you want an expansion so badly?" she asked. "Are you having financial troubles? Because expanding generally doesn't help. Or is it something else?"

Mandy found herself tearing up. "I want to marry Frankie. But ..." She had to fight back the emotion, feeling as though somewhere along the line she'd failed herself. Failed Frankie.

"Then why don't you do it?"

"Because I want to pay my share."

"Of what? A wedding?"

"Yes." It seemed silly using that as an excuse to push Frankie away, but she needed the space to try and sprint ahead so she could be an equal sooner. She'd already taken so much from him over the past year, how could she possibly take more?

"You want a big wedding?"

"Frankie probably does."

"You don't even know?"

"Well…"

"You silly woman, at least ask him if he wants a big celebration before you go killing yourself trying to earn enough to pay for one. And an expansion isn't your answer. They take a lot of money before you ever see any of it back—assuming you ever do. You'd be waiting years for your big wedding. Congratulations, by the way."

"For what?"

"Your engagement."

"We're not engaged."

Blair roared with laughter and Mandy could picture the woman's heavy jewelry jingling with the action. "Are you kidding me? You're not even engaged yet and you're worrying about what's down the road?"

"He asked me to move in with him and I know that after that comes a ring and then a wedding."

"And then kids. A bigger vehicle which is more practical than that souped up truck of yours. Then a bigger house." Blair sighed. "Don't let the future keep you from having what you want today. Not when it comes between you and your man. Don't lose him in the what ifs. If you wait to have enough money, you'll never get married and start a family. He's a good man, the type who will always be right by your side."

"You make it sound so simple."

"When it comes to love, it is simple. It's the one thing in life that always is as long as you don't let your mind get in the way."

MANDY TOOK one last look at the day's receipts and tallied the income, adding it to an ongoing spreadsheet. She popped the month's numbers into a graph and sat back to admire how the green profit line stayed on a steady upward curve. Almost every single day she turned a profit. She was finally coming out ahead. Little by little.

That was good. And today had been especially good.

She opened the folder containing the proposed expansion plans. The ladies had been right. It would have been too much, costing her what she was already short on. Time, money, and energy. Things would have been so tight that one little hiccup would have threatened to send her into receivership.

She sighed and closed the folder. Spying the offer from Hungry Man, she tugged it closer. A chance for more profit with less risk. Delivery could be as simple or as complicated as she wanted it to be. Packaging—a fun new challenge. Baking—it was what she did best. And why not branch out from what she was already doing well?

Frankie had been right. As usual. She could do this.

And honestly, did she and Frankie really, and truly need a big wedding so long as they were together? The town could get over not being to their small, private ceremony. Or they could elope for all she cared. She wanted Frankie. He wanted her. The rest was details. Details that could be worked out when they came to them.

Grabbing her coat to go meet Frankie, she found him already letting himself in.

"Ready to go?" he asked.

With a bounce in her step, she nodded.

"You're so gorgeous in that dress I may have to take you home instead of to the dance."

Laughing, Mandy allowed him to help her into her coat and

locked the restaurant. Snowflakes fell gently as they made their way to the community center.

"I'll go anywhere as long as you're there, Frankie," she said, leaning against him.

"Well, I'm not in Timbuktu or wherever you want to expand to."

"I'm not expanding. I'm staying here. With you. But I might take that brownie deal. What do you think of that?"

"It sounds smart."

"Thank you. I'm hoping it will mean more time with you, but also more profits to pay things off. But I'll probably never be rich, Frankie."

"Me neither."

Inside the warm hall, Frankie checked their coats before leading her onto the dance floor. It seemed half the town had turned out to move to the music and celebrate Valentine's Day.

Frankie held her tight and she clung to him, wanting to tell him that all she really needed at the end of every day was him. She'd been a fool thinking she needed her life to be perfect and problem-free before she could truly be with him. He'd come to her when she'd needed him the most and he would always accept and love her so long as she didn't push him away.

She held him close, relieved she'd come to her senses before she lost him. As they danced, the rest of the dancers blurred into the background and she leaned into him, borrowing his strength.

"Will you love me even if I don't have a lot to offer?" she asked.

He pulled away to look at her. "You have so much to offer, Mandy. Always have."

"Financially."

He laughed. "You're a goof. You know that? I'd love you even if you gambled all of my money away."

"I would never do that to you." Her arms around his neck, she absorbed his heat, staring into his eyes, hoping he'd see all the love she had for him.

"Mandy, we need to talk."

She swallowed, knowing that this moment was an incredibly important one and that she could mess it up if she didn't pause to think about her responses. This was about them. About Frankie. Not her insecurities or business.

"I love you," she blurted and Frankie gave her a small smile, distraction and worry drawing his brows together.

He reached into his pocket, revealing a sparkling ring as he dropped onto one knee. Dancers around them turned to watch and Mandy laughed, feeling free and more delighted than she could ever imagine.

They had immense amounts of love. What more did they need?

She fell into his arms, face snuggled into his neck. "Yes, Frankie. Yes."

He held her away from him slightly so he could deliver his lines while looking her steadily in the eye.

"Mandy, you have been my best friend since the day you walked into gym class, threw your gorgeous hair over your shoulder and told me you'd race me to the top of the rope."

"I remember that. You had the cutest butt in the world. Still do."

"Mandy, will you do me the honor of becoming my wife?"

"Does it have to be a big wedding?"

His brows pinched again. "Uh. I'm a guy," he said hesitantly.

"No?"

"No."

"Then, my dear Frankie …" She paused, looking down as though in regret. "I am going to have to give you a resounding yes." She met his joyful gaze and launched herself back into his arms, almost knocking him over. He pulled her body tight to his as they stood, locked together as though they'd never let go.

The crowd around them cheered as they kissed like the world would never end.

"I love you, Frankie."

"I love you, too, woman. Be mine today and forever."

"Always."

The End

III

VODKA AND CHOCOLATE HEARTS

VODKA AND CHOCOLATE HEARTS

Valentine's Day roared in like a hurricane, with the single women of Blueberry Springs battening down the hatches to protect themselves from the stormy brunt of the despised celebration, and the well-intentioned, if not misplaced, sympathy. But for once, Amber Thompson had someone. And not just *any* someone. She had Russell Peaks, award-winning newscaster from the big city. A man who had been shot in the leg while getting the story, and sported a sexy limp as evidence of his dedication. He was larger than life. Gregarious. Handsome. And soon to be a published author. But most of all, he was hers.

All hers.

Now if only she could get him to quit working so hard on his book's prelaunch and stay home, she could put that little whisper in the back of her mind to rest. The one that told her Russell was spending more time in the city not because of his upcoming book, but because he had grown bored with her. That he was putting distance between them so she'd stay behind in Blueberry Springs when he went back to his sublet urban apartment in two months. It didn't help that family and friends kept hinting that something might be up between them since he hadn't been around as often lately. On Amber's less secure days—such as today—she hated to admit that she secretly feared that they were right. Something was up. Something about her was driving her man away.

Although, she was probably just being paranoid. Of course he loved her; they were living together and he hung on her every word as though he might be tested on it later. Today was Valentine's Day and her boyfriend extraordinaire had promised to meet her in the community center for the town's first annual Love Extravaganza. All day long they would hang out as a couple, perfectly in love, and she would finally be able to prove to herself that she was woman enough for a man like him. And after this little competition, which was starting in ten minutes, they would walk away with the title of The Greatest Couple in Blueberry Springs. Easy peasy.

Assuming he broke away from his Saturday morning meetings to make it back to town in time.

***

Okay, so Amber had to admit that the battle for the Greatest Couple might not be going so well for her and Russell. Mostly because he was still in the semi-near city of Dakota and not in Blueberry Springs.

She smiled and nodded at her friend Beth, who was waving her onto the stage for the second heat of the challenge. Beth and her husband were defending their new title—won from from her sister during an engagement party last year—and probably the biggest contender for the finals. "Come on!" her pregnant friend called, her brown curls bouncing.

Amber held up a finger and hissed into her phone, leaving a message for Russell. "I'm at the community center. We're supposed to go onstage and knock Beth from her throne. With the contest being tied to the festival this year there's actually a prize and she's acting like she's already won it. Where are you?" Amber took a deep breath, trying hard to not sound as if she was an insecure and desperate girlfriend. "Um, happy Valentine's Day. Again."

Where was he, and why wasn't he answering his messages? He used to always pick up, even when in the middle of something important.

"Is Russell here?" asked Nicola Samuels, the festival organizer and town's new community planner. The microphone was to her mouth, the whole community center in on her end of the conversation.

"He's just a bit delayed," Amber replied.

A murmur rose up from the seated audience, and sympathetic looks oozed her way. Yeah, yeah, nice of them to feel for her, but they didn't have to show it.

"Should we proceed without you?" Nicola asked, her palm over the microphone this time.

Amber held up a hand again, scanning the crowd. She caught the reassuring eye of John Abcott, the town lawyer who was pretty much her life's only father figure—which was comforting seeing as she had no clue who her father was. Even the gossip mill didn't have the answer to that one. John raised his brows as if to say, *Anything I can do to help?* She gave a small shake of her head and kept searching for Russell. He could be here, his phone stuck on silent. He could be trying to find her, desperate to illustrate what a sweet and doting boyfriend he was.

When Nicola looked at her for a final answer, Amber shrugged and sadly shook her head. No Russell.

Her phone buzzed as Nicola got the round underway and Amber jumped, clapping the device to her ear. She shut out the applause as Beth and her hubby took the lead. They were already one point ahead of Beth's sister and brother-in-law, driving the crowd wild as the siblings got competitive.

"Amber, babe, honey. I'm so sorry I didn't pick up." It was Russell. Beautiful, handsome Russell. He sounded out of breath and distracted.

"Hey, it's okay," she said, moving around the stage so she was behind the speakers and away from the noise so she could hear him better.

"I was getting new head shots. They did a focus group with librarians who thought mine were too pompous. The new ones are very casual. Kind of sexy, actually."

"How could they not be?" Amber purred.

Her heart warmed as he laughed. "I think the public will be much more receptive to these."

"They'd have to be crazy not to."

"You're such a babe."

"Am I going to need to move to somewhere more private?" she teased. Russell laughed again, low and rich, sending tremors of anticipation up her spine. Why ever had she found a reason to be paranoid? Just because he hadn't used the pronoun *we* when talking about moving back to his old apartment it didn't mean he wasn't mentally including her in his plans.

"You know," she began, "if they'd just listened to me in the first place, you wouldn't have to keep redoing all this promo stuff." She might only be a mail-order database flunky, but some of this marketing stuff seemed pretty obvious to her.

"You don't realize just how much this book couldn't have happened without you, babe."

"Now you're just blowing sunshine. I haven't done a thing." She toyed with the zipper on her jacket. "So? Can you come out now?" The note of hope in her voice was embarrassing. "I have tickets for the dance tonight, as well as reserved a spot for us at the couples skating and picnic, which starts in two hours. If you hurry, you can still make it."

Russell hesitated before replying, and Amber swallowed her growing disappointment.

"Sorry, babe. I really am. But you know how it is. Once I get these guys to pay attention to little ol' me I have to hog them. Publicity wants to brainstorm virtual tours this afternoon." He gave an uncertain laugh and she could picture him running a hand through his sandy hair. "I have no idea what that is."

"When do you think you'll make it out?" Amber struggled to keep the whine from her voice. A warm hand touched her elbow and she turned, relaxing. Her best friend, Scott. Always there when she needed a pal.

Scott gave her a quick peck on the cheek and held out a corsage.

She mouthed, *"Thanks."* Russell was supposed to have bought her one to show Blueberry Springs that she was taken. Instead, her best friend was picking up her boyfriend's slack. What was her world coming to?

"I'll be at the dance for sure, okay, babe?"

"I love you."

"Gotta run. Bye."

Amber slipped her phone into her coat pocket, a mix of emotions warring within her. Russell had called her back right away. That was good. He was still playful and fun. No reason to freak out. So, stop freaking out, right?

Right.

Chill pill taken. It was all going to be okay.

Smiling again, she tapped Scott on his uniformed shoulder. He'd filled out since she'd left town after their high school graduation, eager to achieve something more than her waitressing mother ever had. And she was getting there. Slowly. But Scott ... he'd definitely changed. Her friend was no longer the shy boy she'd once built forts with, or raced sticks against in the river. He was all man. Blueberry Springs's one and only police officer—hence the uniform on a Saturday. And yet, as sexy and sweet as he was, he was still surprisingly single.

Some things definitely did not compute in this crazy world.

"Thanks for the corsage."

"Mary Alice told me Russell hadn't shown." Mary Alice was the town's biggest gossip. Nothing got by her or her sister and, naturally, neither had this little tidbit, which made Amber worry they might see what she feared—that something wasn't right between her and Russell. "Any word on when His Majesty will show up?"

"Don't be a jerk, Scott. He's busy and important."

"I know. It was a joke, Amber." Scott's eyes had that serious look they often did when he was wrestling with something. He opened the corsage box and fumbled with the pin. The look was gone when he shot her a wink as he fastened on the cluster of miniature roses. "We don't want Nicola trying to set you up with Devon Mattson."

"I could handle him." Her friend Mandy's eldest brother was a daredevil. Always had been and always would be. It ran in the family, and even Mandy, who owned one of the town's best restaurants, was a daredevil in her souped up 4x4. She had found romance, but Devon was likely going to have a tougher time.

The crowd grew quiet and Amber peered around the edge of the stage to see what was going on. Devon was down on one knee, pleading with Nicola.

"What is he doing?" Amber asked.

"He's proposing," Scott replied simply.

"Looks like you won't need to worry about the eldest Mattson, after all, Officer Malone. Think she'll go for him?"

"Not a chance. He's in it for the money."

"She's rich?" Amber sized up the town's newcomer with fresh eyes. She'd never pegged Mary Alice's niece as a trust fund kind of gal. And honestly, if Nicola were, her aunts would have had that news up and down Main Street in no time.

"She put out a challenge," Scott was saying. "Whichever new couple gets engaged today wins five hundred dollars worth of Blueberry Springs gift cards—valid in any store in town."

"How new do they have to be?"

"I'm not sure." Scott seemed uncomfortable.

Amber could totally propose to Russell today. That would put her worries to rest once and for all because you didn't leave your fiancée behind, now did you? And the extra five hundred bucks would come in handy.

"I think you two may have been together too long," Scott said, as if reading her mind. He cleared his throat, apparently unable to meet her eye. "Living together and all."

"Oh." Well, still. Getting engaged would be nice—prize or not.

"Amber, over here." Her friend Jen Kulak called them over. She was wearing a red T-shirt that had a heart on the left sleeve and said This Is Me Wearing My Heart On My Sleeve.

Ever the romantic. Had to be another Jen creation.

"This guy does computer stuff like you. And he lives over in Derbyshire." Jen tugged an obviously reluctant man closer.

"I only use a computer for work," Amber replied.

"I thought you were a techie or something? A tele-something," her friend said.

"I tele*commute*." Not a computer wizard whatsoever unless you counted turning the computer off, then on again to resolve any issues, wizardry. "Work from home. Using a computer. It's a mail-order thing. Databases and such."

The tech guy was sizing her up. He might work at a desk, but definitely found his way to the gym. He was strong, built. Totally yummalicious.

Scott's hand settled on Amber's elbow. "She's taken, actually."

"What? You two are dating?" Jen beamed at them.

"No," Amber said a little too forcefully. "Russell. I'm with Russell. Still." Did her friend think she shouldn't stay with him? Did she see something, too?

"Oh, right." Jen glanced away, her eyes drawn back to Scott's possessive hand on Amber's arm. "Sorry."

"I'm actually going to go and—" Amber's phone lit up with

Russell's number. "Sorry! Just have to chat with my boyfriend. Valentine's Day and all." She stepped aside to take the call. The man had impeccable timing.

"Where did you put my computer cord?" he asked.

"Um, what?" Amber glanced behind her and noticed that everyone was eavesdropping. She lowered her voice. "I put it in your bag when you were done working last night. Are you on your way?"

"What? Oh, right. Yeah. Tonight for the thing. The dance. Oh, crap. I was supposed to get you a corsage to show you weren't single. Amber, I'm such a … I'm sorry."

"It's okay." Her voice was betraying her, hollering out that it wasn't okay and that she was falling apart. She could feel her insecurities crowding her, circling in for an upcoming attack where they would wrestle her to the ground, knocking her into an endless spiral of despair lined with double-chocolate-chunk ice cream and tidal wave tears.

"You sure?" Russell asked.

"Yeah, of course." She took a deep breath. Him being busy did *not* mean he didn't love her. She needed to get a grip or her needy, insecure side was going to drive him away for sure. "Scott got me a corsage when he heard you weren't here yet. So it's all good."

"Scott?" There was something odd in Russell's voice. He let out a long breath and his tone changed to one almost like relief. "Good. Good. I'm glad he's there."

"Yeah." She turned to size up her hunky BFF. "He's a good friend."

"Babe?"

"Yeah?"

"I really can't find the cord. It's not in my bag."

"I put it in there and then didn't touch it." She lowered her voice, feeling playful. "But I can touch other cords if you'd like."

Russell laughed. "I may have to ditch all of these meetings and hustle over to your little town."

"Please do. You don't know what you're missing."

"I think I have a pretty good idea."

"Good." Amber grinned as she clicked off the phone.

Scott grabbed her elbow again and propelled her onto the stage. She turned, trying to push her way past him. "What are you doing? They're holding a competition!"

He was big. Tall. And totally blocking her only exit.

"Scott!" She smacked his chest.

"Come on. Let's show these old married bats a thing or two."

"We're not a couple. We have nothing to show them."

"Who cares? Let's have some fun and turn that frown upside down." He gave her a goofy pout and she laughed, allowing him to succeed in forcing her butt into one of the plastic chairs on the temporary stage. The crowd roared their approval and Amber played it up with an exaggerated shrug. Scott was a show-off and was acting as though this was their high school rendition of *Romeo and Juliet* all over again. He was pushing her around and driving the audience wild. Pulling out his handcuffs, he pretended to lock her to the chair.

Cute.

Real cute.

"Scott. Come on. This is for couples."

"That's rather discriminatory." He polished his badge with the cuff of his shirt and raised an eyebrow to the crowd. "Can we play?" he called out. The audience cheered and clapped in response.

Amber laughed and gave in. "Fine. If you think we can take them, let's go."

Nicola, who had been giving them hesitant glances, cleared her throat and tapped her index cards on the lectern. "We have our four couples squaring off for the final heat."

"*Final* heat?" Amber whispered to Scott.

"One couple bowed out, leaving an empty spot. Nicola said we could challenge the leaders." He grinned as he plunked himself in the chair beside Amber, draping an arm across her shoulders. She shoved him off, but he only grinned wider, while the audience chuckled at their shenanigans, clearly thinking it was all an act.

Nicola cast them another furtive look and Amber gave her a tiny shrug.

"Unless our reigning champs—yes, this competition has lived on longer than this festival and has been a game played at engagement parties—are beaten in this round, they will continue to hold the title of The Greatest Couple in Blueberry Springs," Nicola announced. "They will also walk away with a hundred-dollar gift certificate to Benny's Big Burger."

"You're doing this for food?" Amber asked Scott.

"I'm a growing boy. I need a lot of calories."

That was true. Her friend had turned into a brick wall of muscle and manhood, and probably used more calories per day than she consumed in a week. Okay, that was a lie. One look at her hips and generous midriff told the real story of her own daily caloric intake. But if she and Scott weren't best friends, and if she wasn't living with another guy, she might make a play for him.

Oh, wow. She really needed to think about something besides Scott's hot body or she was going to have fantasies about his strong arms, and then she'd never be able to look at him again.

She absently scrawled her answers to the questions written on the index cards provided by Nicola. Amber's responses would need to match up with Scott's verbal ones in order to earn a point. No problem; they'd been friends forever and he could read her mind as though it was his own.

"First question," Nicola announced, after she'd collected the women's cards. "If your girlfriend/wife could do anything in the world, what would it be?"

"Have another healthy baby," Beth's husband replied. A point for them. That was lame. She was already expecting.

"Expand her restaurant," Mandy's boyfriend replied.

"Of course. Everyone knows that. These are so obvious," Amber muttered.

"No talking," Nicola warned. "Scott? Your turn to answer."

Amber had a moment of panic. The only thing she really wanted right now was to feel secure in her relationship. What had she written down? Surely not that?

Scott met her eyes and she froze.

"Learn to fly a floatplane," he replied, his expression giving nothing away.

"How did you know that?" Amber squeaked. She hadn't told a soul about that. Not even Russell.

Nicola frowned. "Not what we have as her answer. Sorry, no point."

"Okay." Amber placed her palms on her thighs and pushed herself up. "Well, I'm done."

"Don't be a sore loser." Scott grasped her hand, keeping her from escaping. The crowd booed her.

"How am I the villain? I have a boyfriend who I'm totally in love with." She pointed to Scott. "And it's not him."

"Aw, come on," he said, patting the seat beside him. "Everyone knows we're only friends."

Members of the audience nodded. Traitors.

Amber sat reluctantly, arms crossed, brow furrowed. She was pretty sure this wasn't how good girlfriends behaved. Maybe Russell would be in the right if he left her behind.

Scott got the next question correct, and the next one. Then they switched to questions about the men. The first was a total gimme.

Best vacation ever? Simple. "When his Grandpa Wes took him to the see the dog show in Dakota for Scott's eleventh birthday.

He had secretly entered Scott's dog, Whiskey, who won. Technically not a vacation, but that's what Scott would answer."

Her best friend smiled fondly. "You remember that?"

"You didn't stop talking about it. Ever."

He laughed as Nicola gave them the point. One point behind Beth. Two questions left.

Amber got them both right. So did her friend.

"Runners-up for this round are Scott and Amber." The two of them stood. "However, word on the street says they are not a couple, and therefore they're disqualified." Nicola took the offered bouquet and handed it to the third-place couple.

"Rip-off!" Amber said to Scott. The indignity. They'd almost won those flowers fair and square. "And I can't believe you tried to scam your way into winning that couples contest, Officer Malone. Whatever happened to upholding the law?"

"Don't make me come over there," he taunted, one hand on his holster as she made her way toward the edge of the stage. "I've seen you speed through town."

She spun and squared off with him. "I'd like to see you try and catch me, *Officer*."

The audience rooted for Scott, encouraging him to lunge at her, knocking her windless as he swept her over his shoulder and off the stage amid hoots and hollers from the town.

"Amber?" Trey, a local teen, asked as Scott put her down. "These are for you." He held up a bouquet of roses.

"But we didn't win," she said with a laugh, shoving Scott away as he tried to mess up her hair.

"They're from Russell. And he says thanks for the dancing, singing guy dressed up as a bear."

"Oh, um, right." Amber accepted the roses, her laughter dying.

Russell. She'd almost forgotten about him.

She buried her nose in the flowers and turned to ask Scott what he was doing next only to find him being whisked away by several of Blueberry Springs's most eligible bachelorettes.

Alone again to battle Valentine's Day as though she was a single woman living in a couples' world. Great. Just great.

———

AMBER WOVE her way through the departing audience, head down. Suddenly wanting nothing more than a few moments to straighten out her thoughts and feelings, she hurried around the first corner she could find.

"Oh, Amber!" Mary Alice, the local gossip, snagged her. She spread out her arms for a big, warm hug that smelled of cigarettes. It was surprisingly good. Must be the woman's massive bosom—nice and cushiony and with no hint of the tin of mints she usually kept hidden in her bra. "You and Scott make such a cute couple." Mary Alice pinched Amber's cheek, her eyes glowing with mischief.

"We're not a couple. I'm with Russell." She waved the red roses, which had gotten slightly squished in the embrace. "And he's going to be here soon."

"Mmm. He's such a steamy hunk of man, you lucky gal. Tell him I say hi, and to save me a turn or two around the dance floor tonight."

"I will."

"It looked like you and Scott had fun though?" The woman raised an eyebrow, a slight smile on her lips as if she knew something Amber didn't.

Amber smiled guiltily. She should have been up there with Russell, not Scott.

"Yeah, fun." She excused herself and hurried away. She needed to sit down with a drink and get herself sorted out. Being with Scott was easy, because he was her best friend, nothing more.

Making her way outdoors, she slipped down the snowy sidewalks to Brew Babies, where she pulled up a tall stool. Moe, who was tending bar, took one look at her and slid a shot of vodka her way. "On the house. Looks like you could use it."

"Thanks," she said, before quickly downing the contents and passing back the glass.

"Another?"

"No, thanks." She took in her surroundings. Oh, heck. She was in the middle of the couples' darts and billiards competition. She couldn't get away from this stupid holiday.

It was supposed to be different this year. Much different.

A stud muffin of a man dressed as Cupid strode by, an intricate "Mother" tattoo on his bicep catching Amber's eye as he paused, turned and flexed, pretending to shoot her with an arrow.

She blinked and turned to Moe who was laughing as he dried a glass. She did not just see that hunky-monkey showcasing all the heavens had offered him in the genetic raffle. Too bad he was going to freeze his junk off as soon as he stepped outdoors without a coat. What a waste. She totally could have set him up with someone who'd appreciate all that buffness.

She rubbed her eyes and stole a second peek at Cupid. Firm butt. Shiny bald, super sexy head, and a crazy set of wings. Yep, he needed someone to set him up with someone who would encourage him not to wear getups in public. But not herself, of course, because this year she didn't need Cupid. However, her friend Scott did. Why was he even still single? He was such a catch.

The thought of not needing Cupid for herself, but for Scott, was more bothersome than she figured it should be. Before she could sort out why, a familiar male voice asked, "How's Blueberry Springs's funnest gal?"

She turned to see John smiling as he sat down beside her, polishing his fogged up reading glasses on his collared shirt.

"Fun and on the loose," she replied before ordering him a

shot. Always just one shot of vodka. Never a beer or anything else.

"Thanks." He tipped the drink into his mouth. "Know what goes well with vodka shots?"

"Salted nuts." Amber tugged the bowl over.

"You got that right."

They sat in silence, munching away as they watched the darts competition going on behind them via the bar's long mirror.

"Bar nuts have the highest fecal matter of any food," she said finally.

John pushed the bowl away and ordered another shot, giving her a sidelong, disgusted look. "To sterilize my mouth."

Amber laughed, ordering one for herself, as well. There was something so comfortable and familiar about John. She could sit for hours with him even though he was as old as her mom. And the way he'd helped out her friends with some pro bono work was pretty cool, too. Not bad for an old guy. If she had to choose anyone she knew to be her secret father, it would be him. Too bad he already had a family.

"Nice flowers," he said, glancing at her roses.

"Thanks."

"Russell treating you right?"

She paused to think about it, then smiled. "I'd love for him to spend more time with me, of course—he's been so busy. But yeah, he's treating me well." And really, gave her no valid reason to be so worried about their relationship. What a silly goose she was.

John watched her for a second as though ready to jump to her defense, then seemingly satisfied with her reply, relaxed. "Glad to hear it."

Scott took the free seat on her other side, ordering himself a draft. "Thought I might find you here."

"Stalking me, are you? Couldn't stay away from me, my quick wit, and supersoft sexy thighs?"

Scott rolled his eyes. "Just thought you might want a friend before you fell into a destructive cycle of self-hate, but I can see you're already on your way. Kudos." He tipped his glass toward her empty shot in a toasting motion. "Hey, John," he added over her head.

"Scott." John gave him a nod and turned to chat with Moe about which lunch specials were least likely to give him a premature heart attack.

"I can't believe you have the audacity to still call yourself a friend." Amber poked Scott in the arm, hurting her finger in the process. "Ow. What are you made of? Steel?"

He grinned and took a sip of his beer, watching her over the glass's rim.

Shaking her head, she continued. "Especially after offering no apologies for the way you made half the town think we're a couple. What is Russell going to think when he finds out?"

Scott tapped the bar with his index fingers, brow furrowed. "Nah. You guys are tight, he'll understand we were just playing around."

Amber watched her friend in the mirror. For whatever reason, she always felt as though she was at her best around Scott and she could never become truly upset with him. It had been that way ever since he'd joined their class back when they were kids.

Scott curved his lower lip over his top one to suck the beer foam from where his mustache used to be. Amber had always thought that was a sexy move. Too bad Russell didn't drink beer. However, if he did, the man wouldn't even have a chance to figure out what had hit him before she took him down due to that sexy lip move.

"He'll understand, Amber. I'm sure of it." Scott gave her a steady look. It was the "it will all be okay" gaze he always sent her when she got muddled up in her head. She gently placed her hand over his, giving it a squeeze. There was nothing in the world like a best friend.

"Hungry?" Moe asked, stopping in front of them. "We have a couple's special on the nachos."

"Very funny, Moe. And just so you know, Russell and I are going to dance in your single face all night." Because for once, she had a boyfriend and things were good.

RUSSELL WASN'T COMING. The dance was almost half over and there was still no sign of her boyfriend. Every worst fear about herself that Amber kept stuffed inside was fighting to pop out.

"Where's that man of yours hiding?" Mary Alice asked, one hand held lightly against her throat. "You didn't scare him off, did you?"

"I'm sure he'll be here soon."

"That's what you said a few hours ago." Mary Alice assessed her, then wrapped an arm around her. "There's not something wrong, is there? I haven't seen that man of yours in weeks."

Amber clutched her drooping bouquet of roses, which she'd been carrying around for hours. Did everyone think he'd left her, and she had been fake-boyfriending her way through Valentine's Day?

"It's all fine. Thanks for asking," she chirped, handing Mary Alice off to her husband, who was waiting to have the next dance.

Embarrassed, Amber walked to the trash and chucked the wilted bouquet. She should go home. The happy couples holding each other, confident in their love as they swayed to the music, were starting to get to her in a way that was going to make her break down. The kind of water main disaster that even a plumber couldn't fix.

Amber moved into the community center's lobby, unable to completely abandon her hopes, but needing to add a sound-muffling barrier between her and the sweet love songs' lyrics that refused to leave her alone.

Sagging into an armchair, she buried her head in her hands, glad nobody was around. She knew she shouldn't expect so much from Russell. He was busy, but he loved her. It would all be okay.

However, it was Valentine's Day. She should be allowed to expect something more than the stereotypical gift of flowers from the man she was living with, shouldn't she?

A puff of cold air fresh from the outdoors washed over her, and expecting her boyfriend, she looked up.

Scott.

A tear trickled down her cheek, but before she could register a thing, Scott had effortlessly scooped her into his arms, hugging her tight. He smoothed her hair, making her chest ache from holding it all in.

"He's a fool for not being here."

Amber wiggled out of her friend's grasp. "He still loves me." Her voice betrayed her, wobbling with uncertainty.

"What's not to love?" Scott gave her a fond chuck on the chin.

"Everyone—" she pointed to the closed doors to the hall, "—thinks he doesn't love me and he's going to ..." She couldn't get the words out.

"Hey, don't go there. Nobody thinks that. Everyone around here just likes to snoop in someone else's business from time to time, okay?" Scott rubbed her arms. "As long as you love Russell and know that he loves you, it doesn't matter what anyone else thinks."

"I know, but he's not coming and it looks like I'm faking the whole relationship. I said he was coming."

"Since when did you care about what everyone else thinks?"

She didn't answer. It was a pretty good question.

Scott dropped his hands onto his hips, sending her a look he'd give kids who got busted egging houses. "And why do I get the feeling that you're hinting for permission to go run home and hide?"

"Can I?"

"No. Come on." He dragged her into the dance hall. "You're going to smile and not show a tiny speck of doubt. You're strong, beautiful, and madly in love with a man who loves you back."

Amber placed her hand in her friend's and allowed him to dance her through the crowd. As long as she had Scott, everything would be okay, even when her love life didn't go the way she'd planned and got the best of her confidence.

It was the second last song and Russell still hadn't shown. No phone call. Nothing.

Amber's feet hurt almost as much as her pride. Scott had stayed by her side, making sure she kept up her game face and acted as though the day hadn't worn a hole in her heart. But he had been stolen away from her for the past three songs, and Amber was feeling her bravado fade like a white shirt's brightness in a load of darks.

She should duck out now in order to save herself from the humiliation of standing alone for the last song, which was always a long, slow one. The way people were pairing up as the dance moved toward the end, she knew there was a very good possibility she'd soon be the only person left on the sidelines.

Sad. Alone. Pathetic.

Definitely feeling uncool, but she could avoid it all by sneaking out while she still possessed a shred of dignity. She could go home and wait for Russell in something lacy and exciting. Maybe buy herself a box of heart shaped chocolates to eat while she waited.

All eyes turned to her as she considered the nearest exit. She froze, certain that everyone had noticed she was the only one not partnered up and about to bolt.

The DJ was saying something over the loudspeaker. Russell. He'd mentioned Russell. Amber turned to check the doorway. Nope, no boyfriend in sight.

Their song. The DJ was playing their song! Russell had called to relay his apology for not making it, and had requested "Make You Feel My Love." Russell loved her. Everything, as usual, had all been in her silly, screwed-up head.

Amber almost fell to the floor in relief. She'd never loved a man more.

It was going to be okay.

She smiled and waved to Mandy and her boyfriend, who were swaying slowly to Adele's rich voice.

As more couples moved by, only then did it hit Amber—she couldn't dance to her own song unless she did it alone. She was the only one on the sidelines.

Just as she turned to go hide in the washroom, Scott appeared. He held out his hand, then pulled her into the throng, his body a comforting shield. She leaned her head against his shoulder. His movements were stiff for a second before his body curved around hers, bringing her closer.

"I couldn't let you dance to your song all alone. Not on Valentine's Day."

Through a throat tight with gratitude, she whispered, "Thanks."

"What are friends for?"

She tipped her head back, feeling such a rush of love for him she wanted to kiss him, to make him as happy as he always made her. "We're a fine team, Officer Malone."

The room around them faded and Amber leaned in, her lips an inhalation from his. Adele sang about warm embraces, the words weaving their way through Amber's mind, seducing her.

Until, abruptly, she blinked and jerked back, causing them to stumble into the couple behind them.

She'd almost kissed her best friend. She turned away, breaking their embrace as she lifted her fingers to her lips.

Life had almost gotten incredibly messy.

Attention on the dance floor pivoted to the couple beside them, where an engagement ring was being held out as an offering for Mandy, who promptly laughed and fell into her man's arms.

Amber swallowed her jealousy, happy for her friend.

"Mandy," he said, "you have been my best friend since the day you walked into gym class, threw your gorgeous hair over your shoulder and told me you'd race me to the top of the rope."

Scott whispered in Amber's hair, the heat of his body warming her back. "You have been my best friend since my first day in Blueberry Springs, sixteen years ago."

"Valentine's Day." She tipped her head to watch him over her shoulder. That made today an anniversary.

"I had no valentines, as the new kid, and you stayed in during recess to make me a card." He wrapped his arms around her, squeezing her tight. "I still have it, you know."

"You do?" She didn't know whether to wiggle out of the embrace or enjoy its strength. But if Russell saw them, she knew it wouldn't be okay. It shouldn't be okay, period. The problem was, it felt as though this was what she'd been missing for months.

She turned in his arms, her hands drifting over his shoulders until they were nested in the short hair at the nape of his neck. Shivers ran down her spine and her heart rate picked up its pace in anticipation.

No. This wasn't cool. It might feel right in this moment, but they were friends. She was living with someone else. Someone good. This was merely her insecure side wanting someone who would validate her.

Scott had to remain nothing more than a friend.

Lowering her arms, Amber gave him a playful shove, her heart breaking when he seemed to take it in stride, his own smile as false as her own. His eyes grew dark as his attention drifted to someone behind her, his right hand moving lightly to his holster.

She turned slowly.

Russell.

He'd come.

"Am I too late to dance with my babe?" Russell asked with a grin, his head cocked.

Amber launched herself into his arms.

The end

Jean Oram is a *New York Times* bestselling romance author. Inspiration for her small town series came from her own upbringing on the Canadian prairies. Although, so far, none of her characters have grown up in an old schoolhouse or worked on a bee farm.

Jean lives outside a small town with her husband and two kids and can often be found outdoors with their big shaggy dog, or writing her next book.

Connect with Jean:

Become an Official Fan: www.facebook.com/groups/jeanoramfans

Goodreads: www.goodreads.com/jeanoram

Newsletter: www.jeanoram.com/FREEBOOK

YouTube: www.youtube.com/AuthorJeanOram

Twitter: www.twitter.com/jeanoram

Facebook: www.facebook.com/JeanOramAuthor

Website & blog: www.jeanoram.com